Three Desperate Women

By Terri Blazell-Wayson

Forward

After food and shelter, our most basic of human needs are to be to be healthy, to be loved, and to be forgiven. Without them, desperation wells up inside of us; hope disappears. Our lives feel out of control and we feel hopeless and worthless.

In the New Testament, there are three women who each had an encounter with Jesus. Three women whose lives, needs and hurts mirror our own journeys. Three women who were desperate for the very things that we are desperate for even today; love, health and forgiveness.

They find it all in Jesus.

Desperate For Healing

In the book of Mark we read the story of a woman who had a bleeding disorder. Not just any bleeding disorder but one that she had been living with for twelve long years.

And a woman was there who had been subject to bleeding for twelve years. She had suffered a great deal under the care of many doctors and had spent all she had, yet instead of getting better she grew worse.[1]

---

[1] Mark 5:25-26

One hundred and forty-four months of a nonstop menstrual cycle. Let me repeat that: *Twelve years. One hundred and forty four months!* Can you imagine how utterly worn out she must have been?

"...yet instead of getting better she grew worse".[2]

Life wasn't easy for women back then. She would rise early to carry heavy pots to the well for water and even heavier ones on the walk back home. Meals were prepared over an open fire in pots she may have formed with her own hands. She ground wheat into flour to make dough and bake into bread. She milked the goats and made cheese. She harvested flax or gathered wool, dyed it and spun it into yarn. She would weave the yarn into cloth before hand-sewing it into clothing for her family. Those same clothes were scrubbed clean on rocks by the river. She swept the packed dirt floors of her home with a handmade broom. All while nursing and raising children.

There was very little leisure time. She would drop into bed at night exhausted only to wake up and do it all over again in the morning.

Days like that would have been exhausting enough without a continuous menstrual flow draining the last bit of energy from her. There were no disposable sanitary napkins. She would have used rags that she washed out and reused over and over again. I can't even imagine it.

The Bible says that she went from doctor to doctor and spent every penny she had but it only got worse. She may have been a young woman when this disease started but twelve years later, it would have made her old beyond her years.

It's possible that this illness was all her children had ever known. Imagine if she had a toddler when the bleeding started. That child would be a teenager when we come to this part in her story. Even if they were older, they would barely remember a mother who wasn't sick. Perhaps this illness left her unable to have children at

---

[2] Mark 5:26

all. To be barren was a great shame in that long-ago society. It was unlikely anyone would marry her and many believed a woman in this condition was cursed by God for something she had done. In other words, it was her fault.

~ This woman knew exhaustion.
She knew shame. She knew loneliness. ~

In those times, anyone with any type of bleeding or discharge was to be isolated. She was not to be around other people at all. She may have worn a covering over her face and the law required that she shout "Unclean" whenever she went out in public.

There was a good reason for this. In a day when medical care was primitive at best, it prevented the mass transmission of diseases. But it also kept the ill isolated and alone often until the day they died. No one to be at their bedside or hold their hand or stroke their hair. Just aloneness.

The bleeding controlled her life – what she did, where she went, who she visited, what she wore.

She may have gotten up extra early to get to the well before anyone else was there just to stay within the rules. Her children and husband would have run errands for her because she couldn't go out. She probably felt shame. Shame that she had this illness she couldn't fix. Shame that her family had to pick up the slack. Shame that she wasn't like the other women. Shame every time she had to say those words, "Unclean."

"...yet instead of getting better she grew worse".[3]

Every single day as she fought to keep it together, her body fought against her, wearing her down more and more.

~ Life has a million different ways of wearing us down. ~

---

[3] Mark 5: 26

Years ago, when I would go camping with my children, they collected small, pretty rocks on our hikes. We bought a stone tumbler to polish them. The tumbler consists of a small barrel that you place the stones in along with water and polishing compound. Then you turn it on and the barrel turns round and round for an entire month. Polishing rocks is not a quick process.

What we noticed after four weeks of anticipation, was that while some rocks polished up into beautiful little treasures, many of the rocks did not survive. As we rinsed away the polishing compound, we also rinsed away the fine grains of sand that had once been a possibility. While they seemed to hold great promise when we first put them in, they were made up of materials that could not survive the stress of constantly being ground down.

Daily life contains many stresses that constantly wear us down – not just for a month but for years on end. Does the stress "polish" us up or tear us apart?

~ What am I made of? ~

Camping Stones

I am being worn away,
ground down
like the stones I pick up and put in my pocket.
I put them in the tumbler
where they smash together
wearing down and eroding away.
They cannot be polished.
I put them in again,
over and over again
but they will not shine.
They contain nothing of value or substance
so they become nothing.
Just like me,
I am being worn away
ground down.
Oh, great God
Find something of substance in me
Before I am gone.

There have been times when I felt that I was being ground down to almost nothing. Times when I thought there really was nothing left. On my own, that would have been the case but when I asked Jesus to be my Savior He became my Rock. A rock that can't be worn down. A rock that can't be moved.

I Samuel 2:2b *"there is no Rock like our God."*

We run to this Rock for shade. We climb into this Rock to protect us. And this Rock is inside of us – the solid Rock that cannot be worn down. His Spirit in us, becomes that unbreakable, unshakeable diamond that can only become more beautiful with time.

Now it is God who makes both us and you stand firm in Christ. He anointed us, set his seal of ownership on us, and put his Spirit in our hearts as a deposit, guaranteeing what is to come.[4]

He adds a "substance" that cannot be worn down or washed away. I didn't always sense it; sometimes I thought I would just disappear; sometimes my prayers were nothing but tears.

How worn down this woman must have been. When she heard there was a Healer in the area, she may have been skeptical. How many times before had someone said there was a miracle worker in town? A charlatan who came through promising health in a bottle of snake oil for the price of her life savings. Faith healers who claimed she just didn't have enough faith. Perhaps she wept and prayed at the temple until the priests were sick of seeing her. Or her friends told her that God was punishing her for her sins.

And now the town is all ablaze over a new Healer. But this One is different they say. He's not selling anything. And the people He healed are people she knew. He touched the sick with His own hands; He wasn't afraid of catching whatever they had. He spoke with love and showed compassion.

---

[4] II Corinthians 1:21-22

Some said that He wasn't just a healer; that He was the Messiah they had been waiting for. Hope rose up in her; hope she didn't know was still there. That was the Rock within her.

When she heard about Jesus, she came up behind him in the crowd and touched his cloak, because she thought, "If I just touch his clothes, I will be healed."[5]

She did something crazy. She went out into the crowd. She did not shout "Unclean." Perhaps she fixed her hair and put a little rouge on her cheeks to cover up her pale, sunken cheeks. She hoped no one would even notice that she was there. She could be stoned for this great act of desperation and defiance.

"If he is for real," maybe she's thinking. *"If He is for real,"* then I don't need rituals or prayers or oils. Just a touch will do. If He's that good, He doesn't even have to know. So she threaded her way through a throng of people, buried her face in her cloak so no one recognized her then reached out a pale, trembling hand, touched the hem of His robe and snatched her hand back so quickly that no one noticed.

For that woman to even be in a place where others gathered was a major offense worthy of stoning. Every single person she came in contact with was considered contaminated. They would have had to put their lives on hold and were required to go into isolation for at least a week living in terror that they now had what she had. Writing this as the words *Coronavirus* and *Monkeypox* jump out from the daily news – it is very relatable. She was putting her life on the line. She was desperate. She may even have been a bit suicidal. Maybe she thought, *"If I get caught and stoned to death at least this misery will be over. Either this man can help me or I may as well die."*

---

[5] Mark 5:27-28

So she quietly, desperately pushed her way through the crowd contaminating everyone she came in contact with. She dared not speak up. If she were recognized, it could literally be the death penalty. The Bible says she was trembling with fear. But she didn't let her fear stop her. Quietly, she reached out and made contact. And her life changed. She knew it. She felt it. It was real.

Immediately, her bleeding stopped and she felt in her body that she was freed from her suffering.[6]

I've heard testimonies like that. People who reached bottom, so desperate. Everything gone. No hope. And they cried out, "God, if you are real – SAVE ME!" And their lives began to change.

Something inside of that woman changed. She could feel it. But so could Someone else.

At once Jesus realized that power had gone out from him. He turned around in the crowd and asked, "Who touched my clothes?" His disciples answered, "You see the people crowding against you and yet you can ask, who touched me?"[7]

His followers were incredulous. They were in a crowd that was pressing around Him from every direction. People were shouting and reaching out. Some were begging for help. Pharisees and Sadducees were interrogating Him. His disciples were surrounding Him like body guards; a hand on His elbow steering Him this way, another on His back steering Him that way.

In Luke 8, one crowd is described as almost crushing Him. They were all like that.

"Who touched me?" Everyone. Everyone touched Him. But Jesus knew the difference.

---

[6] Mark 5:29
[7] Mark 5:30-31

But Jesus kept looking around to see who had done it. Then the woman, knowing what had happened to her, came and fell at his feet and, trembling with fear, told him the whole truth. He said to her, "Daughter, your faith has healed you. Go in peace and be freed from your suffering."[8]

*~ **Jesus knows each of us so uniquely,** **He recognizes us just by our touch.** ~*

This woman who felt all alone in a crowd faced the crowd. This woman who felt different from everyone around her joined in with everyone around her. This woman who felt unloved and unclean was worthy of being loved and being healed.

In II Corinthians 5:17, the Apostle Paul writes, *Therefore, if anyone is in Christ, the new creation has come: The old has gone, the new is here!*

She became a new creation! She probably ran home, grabbed her husband and children and told them all about it. She may have hugged her friends along the way, friends she hadn't been able to see or touch in years; pulling them in tight while they both wept with joy. Or they might have pushed her away; not certain of her claim. They may have heard this before. Perhaps her bleeding stopped for a few days and she thought it was over then it returned; taunting her as the red stain seeped through her garments. But regardless of what anyone thought, she had encountered Jesus - this time she was healed. She was a new person.

---

[8] Mark 5:32-34

Years ago, I had my own bleeding disorder. My menstrual cycle started normally enough. However, as the days passed, it seemed to grow heavier instead of lighter. Three weeks passed without letting up. The weeks turned into a month. I couldn't sleep because no matter how thick the pad, I would soak the sheets during the night. When I was in public, I was constantly running into the restroom to check for accidents. I even had to leave a funeral early because I had soaked through my clothing. I hurried out, humiliated, my sweater tied around my waist, a damp stain on the folding metal chair. Still, I kept thinking it would run its course and go away on its own. [I can be stubborn.]

After another month without relief, I relented and saw my doctor. Several tests later, I was put on medication to make the flow stop, vitamins to increase my iron levels and scheduled for a minor procedure to cauterize blood vessels in my uterus. The procedure went fine and my body returned to normal. I went through four months of uncertainty, discomfort and inconvenience.

This woman in Mark 5 lived like that for twelve years.

Twelve years! I still can't fathom that this had been her life for so long.

There are things in my life that I have been dealing with and praying about for so long. Just like this woman – the years become a decade and then another and I wonder if my prayers are heard or if God even cares.

Then I think about this woman. Jesus did not condemn her for breaking the rules and laws of the day in order to see Him. He did not scold her for being too afraid to meet Him face to face. Instead, He praised her for that tiny shred of faith that still held on after twelve years of suffering. She did not give up. She took one more chance – this time on the One who could truly heal.

John 11 tells us the story of a man name Lazarus. He was the brother of Martha and Mary, beloved friends of Jesus. Lazarus became very ill, close to death, so they did what we all do; they sent a message to Jesus. *"Our brother is sick. Come heal him."*

The message was delivered to Jesus but He ignored it. Read that again - He ignored it.

Jesus, who could heal with a single touch or heal from a distance just by saying the word. Jesus, who could heal anything: blindness, leprosy, paralysis. Nothing was too hard for Him. Martha and Mary were some of His most faithful followers. But He stayed where He was and did nothing.

By the time Jesus arrived at Martha and Mary's house, Lazarus wasn't just dead – he had been buried for four days. That's how long He waited. The sisters are doubly grieved; their brother has died and Jesus inexplicably let them down. Their hope was buried in that tomb with their brother.

Mary and Martha both said the same thing to Him. *"If you had been here, our brother would not have died."*[9]

You might think that the writer of Christian books has it all together. But I do not. And right now I am struggling with some unanswered prayers that sound very much like Martha and Mary.

"Jesus, would you just show up!" I cry. And like Martha and Mary, I grieve for the prayers not answered.

But Jesus does something absurd. He asks to be taken to the grave then tells them to roll the stone away from Lazarus' tomb.

"You don't want to do that," they tell Him. This was the desert. Hot and dry. Things rot quickly. Not a good place for a dead body. They must be buried quickly and you certainly would not reopen the grave any time soon.

"His body has been decaying in there for days. It will stink," they said. But Jesus insisted.

---

[9] John 11:21 & 32

Everyone probably held their breath or held a sleeve over their nose and mouth as a few strong men heaved the stone away from the opening of the tomb. They probably stared silently at the dark, vacant opening. There were rules and laws about touching dead bodies and it looked like Jesus was about to break all of them. They didn't know what Jesus was going to do but one thing is for sure – they weren't expecting what He did next.

Then Jesus shouted, "Lazarus, come out!"[10]

~ And Lazarus walked out of that tomb! ~

When God doesn't answer our prayers *when* we want Him to or *how* we want Him to, it could be His way of preparing us for something more. He is forming us and fashioning us like a potter creates beautiful pottery. We start out as an irregular lump of clay and He forms us with His own hands. It takes time. We don't look perfect during the process – only when He is finished – do we take on the form of what we are to be.

Sometimes, that means prayers go unanswered or things don't turn out the way we want them to. Do not stop believing in God because He has not answered your prayer in your time. Listen to what He says:

This is what the Lord says, "At just the right time, I will respond to you…"[11]

Bring that last shred of hope to the Savior. Grasp His hem. Trust Him that when it seems like it is too late, He has only just begun.

---

[10] John 11:43
[11] Isaiah 49:8a NLT

As I Grasp Your Hem

It's me, Lord
I'm the one
Touching the hem of your robe
Just one touch
I know it will do
Then will come healing
Only from You.

I did not mean to draw your stare
I thought the crowd would hide me well
Yet You found me
Out of all these needy people
You found me.

I kneel trembling at your feet
I don't deserve to be special.
I would have settled
for just Your hem
Yet You love me.

I feel Your gentleness
as you lift me to my feet.
The crowd fades away
This is between You and me
Cleansing cannot come from a robe
Your death, Your blood has bought me
I see that now.

I was without value
And now I am priceless.
Heal my soul
Cleanse my sin
Make me whole
As I grasp Your hem.

Not all bleeding is physical. There is another kind. The kind that comes from grief. It drains us of our strength and leaves us barely functioning. We lose sleep. We lose our purpose for living. We lose our mind. Like physical bleeding, if it goes on for too long, others have to pick up the slack. Family has to pitch in as we struggle. Friends who were supportive at first, stop reaching out, afraid that the grief that is drowning you will drown them too.

And the grieving can be for anything; a loved one dies, a lost job, a broken marriage, a dead pet, a friendship ending. Most of the time we bounce back. We get a new job. We find a new love or a new friend. We adopt another pet. We haven't forgotten what we lost, but we find a new happiness to fill our soul.

Sometimes the grief hangs on. Surround yourself with good friends. Spend time in God's house with God's people. Read the Word and pray. Let Him be the Rock within you. Redirect that grief into something with purpose.

But there is one type of grief we don't get over; the death of a child. It is unnatural. It is unforgettable. It can break us in ways that do not heal. It is the most desperate need for healing there is. Like Lazarus, we must wait until the stone is rolled away and we are on the other side. And we will see our precious one again.

We must believe that whatever God's plan or purpose – no matter how much we don't understand it, that He loves you and He loves your child. He knows your grieving heart. He knows what's wearing you down. Reach out. Touch His hem. Find peace that He has a purpose, even in this.

In Heaven, Children

In heaven, children climb upon God's lap.
They run their fingers through His beard
And weave daisy chains for His hair.
They look into His eyes and smile.
He tickles them and they giggle like little chirping birds.
Stop and listen when birds sing;
It is our children laughing.

In heaven, they reach up and take the hands of angels.
They go for long walks and sail banana leaf boats on Heaven's lake.
They splash the water with their pudgy hands until it splatters
over the sides, down to earth.
Hold out your hands and feel the rain;
It is our children playing.

In heaven, children run barefoot through the warm grass.
They flop down in it with their chins in their hands
While bees buzz about their heads.
Bees never sting in heaven, they only kiss.

The children hold hands in a big circle with God in the middle.
They sing ring-around-the-rosie.
When they all fall down it sounds like thunder.
Smile when it thunders.
It is only God and our children playing.

In heaven, angels tuck our children into the clouds for their naps.
They rock them gently to sleep with the breezes.
When they awaken, it is still day,
For in heaven it is never night.
Close your eyes and feel the wind on your face.
It is rocking our children to sleep.

In heaven, no one ever hurts a child.
Never makes them cry.
In heaven, they are safe
And warm and loved.
It is all they know, for God makes it so.
They call it Home
And play hide-and-seek around God's throne.
Someday we will go there.
Our children will come running out with arms open wide,
Shouting, "ollie ollie oxen, Free!"

Desperate to be Loved

A woman wearily walks across the sand during the hottest part of the day to draw water from a well.

What do we know about her from that simple sentence?

No one likes her.

Women collected water in the morning while it was still cool. They used this time to laugh and talk and socialize. This woman is walking in the brutal heat of noon. She balances a heavy clay pot on her shoulder. Filled with water, it will be even heavier on the way back. She anticipates dipping her scarf in the cool water and rinsing her face; the sweet taste of it on her tongue. A tiny relief in a very hard life. She is already dreading the walk back. She is tired and thirsty and worn out.

She chose the hottest part of the day because no one else would be around. No one went out in this heat. She wanted to avoid the looks, the whispers and most of all, the judgement of those who gather in the cool of the morning. She wanted to be alone. She had probably made this trip many times before. But today would be different. In fact, it will never be the same again.

So He came to a town in Samaria ... and Jesus, tired as he was from the journey, sat down by the well. It was about noon... When a Samaritan woman came to draw water, Jesus said to her, "Will you give me a drink?"[12]

"Will you give me a drink?" Such a simple request yet it would change her world.

"Will you give me a drink?"

Jesus spoke first. He had to. The culture of the day was similar to parts of the Middle East even today. A woman didn't speak to a man. So Jesus spoke to her.

He saw her. He didn't look away or pretend she didn't exist. She was used to those kind of looks. He didn't look at her as though she was sexual prey that He could do what He pleased with. She was used to those kinds of looks, too.

~ *He looked at her as though she mattered.* ~

---

[12] John 4:5, 7

Jesus saw her as a human being and best of all, Jesus recognized her. The Apostle Paul wrote that we were *"chosen in Him before the creation of the world.*[13]*"* Before the earth was a blue dot in our galaxy. Before there was a galaxy. Before time. Jesus already knew each one of us and chose us to be here.

"Before I formed you in the womb I knew you and before you were born I consecrated you."[14]

Imagine His joy at finally seeing her. How excited He must have been to finally speak to her. Jesus didn't come there for water. He came there for her!

He feels that way about you, too. He knows your name, your story, your brokenness and your dreams. You were chosen to be here for that moment when you see Him, really see Him, for the first time. It doesn't matter what your life looks like or how messed up you think it is. It isn't so messed up that He didn't want you here.

Then Jesus asked her for something that she could give. She didn't have much. But she could give Him a cup of cool water. Do you hear Jesus speaking into your life? He will only ask you for something that you can give.

[9] *The Samaritan woman said to him, "You are a Jew and I am a Samaritan woman. How can you ask me for a drink?" (For Jews do not associate with Samaritans.)*

"Jews do not associate with Samaritans."

This Jew does. This Jew talks to Samaritans. This man talks to women. This Rabbi talks to unbelievers. He talks to atheists, Muslims, Buddhists and Egyptians. He talks to sick people, poor people, blind people and helpless people. Anyone with an open heart and even those with closed hearts. He breaks rules and conventions to talk to us, no matter who we are or what we've done.

---

[13] Ephesians 1:4
[14] Jeremiah 1:5

If you know anything about the history of the Jews and Samaritans, it is that they did not get along. They had a nasty, violent history. They hated each other and they avoided each other. Many Jews would walk all the way around Samaria to get to the cities on the other side even if it added days to their journey.

When she saw Jesus sitting there, she may have stopped before she even got to the well. Hesitating, afraid to go on any further; debating in her mind whether she should turn around and go home. Not only frightened by this disruption but perhaps angry; it's hot, it's a long walk back, and she needs water. Everything is ruined.

As far as she's concerned, there is nothing good about this situation. There are a lot of people who encounter Jesus and don't look at it as a good situation. "It costs too much." "It's not real." "I've been hurt before." "Here come those religious fanatics again." "I don't trust you." And on and on.

I picture her standing there with that big pot on her shoulder, eyeing this stranger, partially turned, ready to run back the other way. He's asking for a drink of water but what does He really want?

Jesus answered her, "If you knew the gift of God and who it is that asks you for a drink, you would have asked him and he would have given you living water.[15]"

"Sir," the woman said, "you have nothing to draw with and the well is deep. Where can you get this living water? Are you greater than our father Jacob, who gave us the well and drank from it himself...?[16]"

"Who do you think you are?"

That's what she was saying. Can you imagine saying that to Jesus?

"Who do you think you are?" "You just asked *me* for water! And now you tell me that you have water?"

---

[15] John 4:10
[16] John 4:11-12

"Who do you think you are?" "You have nothing to draw water with."

"Who do you think you are?" "Jacob dug this well. We rely on this well. We know there's water in this well. Where does your water come from? Are you going to make water appear out of nothing?"

How many times have I put my foot in my mouth? How many times have I talked like a no-it-all and embarrassed myself? Or hurt someone. Jesus could have responded in a lot of different ways to put this woman in her place. But He didn't. He was gentle, loving and patient.

Jesus answered, "Everyone who drinks this water will be thirsty again, but whoever drinks the water I give them will never thirst. Indeed, the water I give them will become in them a spring of water welling up to eternal life.[17]"

It's hard to know what she was thinking by now. When Jesus said the water He gives wells up into eternal life, she might have thought He was a magician who held the secret to the Fountain of Youth. All we know is she was intrigued. Instead of running home, she stayed. She edged a little closer. Brought the pot down off her shoulder.

The woman said to him, "Sir, give me this water so that I won't get thirsty and have to keep coming here to draw water.[18]"

She wanted this. She wasn't quite sure what it was. She didn't know Who was offering it. But she wanted it. When we come to Jesus, we don't know everything there is to know about Him. We just know that He has something that we need. If you've never read the Bible and the only thing you know about the name of Jesus is as a swear word, don't let that stop you from asking for what He is offering. He is offering "living water." Water is life. Jesus is offering life. A changed life. A new life. Eternal life. And it's free.

He told her, "Go, call your husband and come back."

---

[17] John 4:13-14
[18] John 4:15

"I have no husband," she replied.

Jesus said to her, "You are right when you say you have no husband. The fact is, you have had five husbands, and the man you now have is not your husband. What you have just said is quite true.[19]"

Suddenly, it got serious. The man offering living water was now going to bring up her living hell.

As the saying goes, then the other shoe drops. Her ugly past makes an appearance front and center. And it wasn't the townspeople pulling back the curtain. It wasn't the women who gather in the morning to gossip. Or the holier-than-thou locals reminding her that she wasn't as good as them. Instead, it was Someone who shouldn't have known anything about her at all. As far as she was concerned, they had never met. How did He know? And look what He knew!

Five husbands. This is significant because in those days, a woman couldn't file for divorce; only the husband could. So she had five husbands who dumped her. They rejected her, probably abused her and abandoned her. This woman was stained. This woman had scars. She probably didn't have many friends. The last thing the other women in town wanted around was a woman who attracted men like a moth to a flame. A woman who would live with any man who came along.

To be honest, I probably wouldn't want her to be my neighbor. One of those couples that are always fighting at all hours of the night. Doors slamming. Walls shaking. Dishes breaking.

On the outside, all the other women saw was a tramp. [I might have thought of her that way too.] But on the inside, the part they couldn't see, was a desperate broken woman. A woman who just wanted someone to love her. She is emotionally battered and beaten down. She is tired. She is lonely. She is an unwanted nobody and she knows it.

---

[19] John 4:16-18

And now this stranger. How far had her reputation spread that this total stranger knew all about her past? And what was this living water he kept talking about. She didn't know it, but a drop of living water was already welling up in her. Her thoughts went in a different direction; one she could never have imagined when she got up that morning.

The woman said, "I know that Messiah…is coming. When he comes, he will explain everything to us.[20]*"*

She was listening. That little kid in Sunday School that you don't think is paying attention? That next door neighbor who laughs at your beliefs. That working mom who is far too busy to make time for church. They're still listening. Show God's love by loving others. Share God's love; not condemnation. You never know who's listening.

She went from a sarcastic "Who do you think you are?" to a mystified "Who ARE you?"

Then Jesus declared, "I, the one speaking to you—I am he.[21]*"*

"I am he." Speaking to her!

He chose her to reveal His majesty. Are you reading this? Then He chose you, too. He has chosen you to hear His voice, to be filled with Living Water and to feel His love.

Then, leaving her water jar, the woman went back to the town…[22]

She left her water jar. She didn't need water from the well right now. Yes, she'll have to go back for it. We live in a physical world. We have physical needs. But at that moment, the Living Water has quenched her thirst and satisfied all of her needs.

---

[20] John 4:25
[21] John 4:26
[22] John 4:28

Jesus chose her to announce His arrival. Not a religious leader, a famous celebrity, a politician or pious member of society. He chose an unworthy, unwanted outcast.

"...the woman went back to the town and said to the people, "Come, see a man who told me everything I ever did. Could this be the Messiah?" They came out of the town and made their way toward him.[23]

The Bible only gives us an edited version of this story but I imagine that this woman and Jesus had a much longer conversation than is recorded. *"He told me everything I ever did."* There was much more. Perhaps they talked about those husbands and what led her to each one. Perhaps she wept as the pain of her past came to the surface but this time instead of scarring her, she felt healing and forgiveness for the first time.

He chose her to spread the good news. He knew everything about her and loved her anyway.

~ *One of the most important messages in the Bible is in this story.* ~

Think about what Jesus could do. He could heal the sick. He could feed thousands of people with a handful of bread. He was constantly surrounded by people with the greatest needs– sick, dying and hungry. Crowds swarmed him morning, noon and night. When he multiplied the bread and fishes there were over 15,000 people there.[24] When the woman with the bleeding disorder touched him, He was described as being crushed in the crowd.[25] He was surrounded by so many people that when they tried to bring a paraplegic to Him for healing, they had to dig a hole in the roof and lower the man down on a hammock in front of Jesus.[26]

And He did important work. He gave sight to the blind. He healed illnesses and he fed the hungry. He even raised the dead!

---

[23] John 4:28b-30
[24] John 14:13-18
[25] Luke 8: 42-47
[26] Mark 2:1-5

But this woman - there was nothing physically wrong with this woman. She was healthy. She was strong. She had her eyesight. She had a roof over her head and food on the table.

~ All she had was a broken heart. ~

Think on that for a minute.

Jesus took the time to slip away from the throngs of needy, desperate people, just to be alone with her. Her broken heart mattered. Most importantly, it mattered to Him. Healing is temporary. Everyone Jesus healed eventually died. Feed someone and they are hungry again. Give them something to drink and they will thirst again. Heal the blind or the lame and old age or illness will close their eyes and weaken their limbs again.

But a heart – that treasure room of your soul and spirit - is the most valuable thing because it will never die. It goes into eternity.

Jesus was waiting there at her well. He looked right down inside her soul. He knew all about her. He talked to her. He did not judge her. He told her that she was still worthwhile. He offered her Living Water. He gave her a new heart.

Several years ago, I was desperate. What I didn't realize was how desperate I had been for most of my life; setting myself up for one disaster after another. Desperation was a family pattern. My parents, my grandparents; who knows how many generations back. They were desperate to survive – they went through two world wars. Desperate for peace. Desperate for hope. Desperate for food. Desperate for safety. They were desperate for love. Desperate for a job. Desperate for a home. Desperate for an income. Desperate for normalcy. Desperate to heal the aching brokenness inside of them. Instead they passed that desperation onto their children and their children's children.

And ultimately to me.

On the outside, I looked just fine. But I lived what I saw growing up; the broken, destructive patterns that were handed down to me like family heirlooms. I told myself that I would never be like that but those patterns and behaviors were imprinted on me. I unconsciously responded like my parents did because this is what I saw and this is what I knew.

It came to a head one summer years ago. Someone that I cared deeply about walked out of my life. At the same time, I miscalculated my bank account and realized I had no money. Forget about paying the mortgage. My credit card balances became mountains.

Even my dog got sick which doesn't sound like much but in the midst of everything else, it was *one more thing!* She got better-$100 later which doesn't go over well when you're living off credit cards, transferring balances to interest-free offers in a wild, topsy-turvy balancing act. My life had fallen apart and there I was - desperate. Desperate for healing, for love and for forgiveness.

I couldn't even tithe. I always patted myself on the back when I put my envelope in the offering plate. But that's when I realized God didn't want my money. He put me in a position of not being able to give Him anything. My Heavenly Father wanted something more.

"I want your heart. That's My heart. I died to save it before you were even born. I watched it grow within you when you were in your mother's womb. And no matter how hard your childhood was, I was still protecting you. I formed you, I shaped you, and I nurtured you. You are Mine. It's time to come back."

I dropped to my knees and confessed my sins and wept and sobbed and confessed some more and I gave my Savior His heart back. Now I'm heartless. People say that like it's a bad thing. But my old heart – it was so selfish and dangerous and ugly, I had to get rid of it. He gave me a new heart.

Now, I have a new kind of desperation. I am desperate to honor Him, desperate to obey Him and desperate to love Him with all my heart. I'm desperate for you to know Him too. You'll never find anyone who loves you more.

But let's go back to the woman at the well. There's one more thing. It's something Jesus said to her when the dreaded topic of her revolving husbands came up.

"You are right when you say you have no husband. The fact is, you have had five husbands, and the man you now have is not your husband. What you have just said is quite true."[27]

Everyone focuses on the five husbands and the man she is living with now. Even today, every sermon I've ever heard about this woman focuses on her past; the husbands, the divorces, the unmarried relationship. This woman probably heard it a lot.

"Pssst, did you hear? Five husbands! The last guy won't even bother marrying her. So pathetic."

When was the last time anyone said something nice to her? When was the last time she heard a compliment?

"It's nice to see you. "You should wear your hair like that more often – it's lovely." "You are so hard working."

Probably more years than she can count. But Jesus, this Jesus who looks on the heart, instead of criticizing her or looking down on her, He sees something good in her. She told the truth in her own way. But Jesus grasped onto that one small thing and complimented her.

"You are right…" "What you have just said is quite true."

How easy it is to criticize. How often we pick at what is wrong and are blinded to the small things that someone is doing right. Jesus promised her Living Water and that one small compliment might have been the first drop she felt on her parched soul.

---

[27] John 4:17-18

Jesus finds the good in us when others don't. He lifts us up instead of putting us down. Let us do the same. Let us offer a cup of cold water in the form of a compliment. Let us emulate the Savior and love in His name.

Jesus knew her deepest, darkest secrets and still thought she was worthy. Worthy of His time. Worthy of His love. He focused on the things that were right in her. And if you are the one that others find fault in, remember that Jesus sees you and knows you. You are worthy, too, no matter who you are or what you've done.

One day, Jesus came and sat down by my well – a dry, parched place only wet by my tears. He brought His own living, loving water to my soul. He died on the cross because His death gave me life. His grace rains down on me and surrounds me so clearly I can almost feel it.

~ I had nothing to offer Him but a broken heart and that's what He wanted most. ~

Everyone has a well – and Jesus is sitting there – waiting. Waiting to give you a changed life, another chance and a new heart.

A New Heart

A new heart,
He's given me a new heart
And the things I used to do
Aren't fun anymore.
The things I used to say
Would make me hang my head in shame
Because my new heart
Is pure.

A new heart,
He's given me a new heart.
And the thoughts I used to think
Have been purged from within.
The plans I used to make
Would make my new heart break
Because my new heart
Knows no sin.

A new heart
He's given me a new heart.
And it floats on a river of peace.
It soars on eagles wings.
It's filled with so many good things
Because my new heart
Belongs to Him.

Desperate for Forgiveness

There is one more desperate woman.

The teachers of the law and the Pharisees brought in a woman caught in adultery. They made her stand before the group and said to Jesus, "Teacher, this woman was caught in the act of adultery. In the Law Moses commanded us to stone such women. Now what do you say?"[28]

---

[28] John 8:3 - 5

She stands all alone in a circle of stones. She stares at her bare feet; the cold, smooth dirt squishing between her toes. She does not look up at the ring of men surrounding her. She knows she's guilty. A breeze slices through the tears in her tunic where she was grabbed and dragged to this place.

~This will be her last day alive. ~

How desperate this woman must have been to commit adultery at a time when you could be stoned to death for it. How miserable and lonely she must have felt. Maybe her husband had a temper. Maybe he treated her like property. Maybe he cheated on her. Maybe it wasn't any of those things; maybe she just didn't feel like she was enough.

She knew what it was like to be alone even as she shared a bed with someone, to cry when no one was looking, to be less than nothing. Then she met somebody who temporarily made her feel like something. So she took the biggest risk of her life and lost.

Even her lover had used her. He did not love her enough to stand by her. She was all alone.

Do you think her friends knew? Do you think they encouraged her? *"Go for it, girlfriend. You only live once!"* Or do you think some of them cautioned her? *"Don't do it! Think about your family, your kids, your life."* Or was the whole thing so under the radar that everyone who knew her was shocked? It didn't matter. She had committed a great sin. Penalty: Death by Stoning.

They were using this question as a trap, in order to have a basis for accusing him.[29]

She did not live in a forgiving society. Even the religious community let her down. They did not care about their laws or see a hurting, broken human being deserving of compassion. Instead, she was just a prop to trap Jesus; the one they called Teacher but did not want to learn from Him. If Jesus called for mercy, He, a rabbi, would

---

[29] John 8:6

be violating the very laws that the Jews lived by including Himself. But if He cried, "She has sinned, stone her!" it voided His message of love and forgiveness that He had spent the last three years preaching.

But Jesus bent down and started to write on the ground with his finger.[30]

We don't know what He wrote. Scholars have debated that for centuries. If it were important, God would have included it.

She stared at her feet and would not look up. A circle of stones surrounded her; some the size of pomegranates, some even larger. Many of the men in the circle already had a rock in their hands, their fidgety fingers squeezing and releasing; anxious to do the deed. Whoever throws the first stone, she hopes it goes right to her head. She wants to go down fast and get it over with. Less pain, she hopes. She squeezes her eyes tight willing herself not to cry. She knew what she was getting into and this was the consequence.

The noise around her seems deafening. Shouting over each other, they question and bait the Teacher. The crowd outside the gates watching from a distance; the ones closer to the front describing the scene to those behind them.

The ones in the back may have shouted, "What's happening?" and those who were closest called out, "They've called for her stoning." Stoning. The words ripple from front to back like a wave; "stoning" reverberating like an echo.

But then it becomes quiet.

"Are they going to start?" she wonders. Her head drops even lower and her shoulders tighten, waiting for the first blow. But it doesn't come. Carefully, she opens her eyes and glances around; only stones and feet in her range of view. And there is the Teacher. He is kneeling down and writing in the dirt. She can see His face. It is calm and loving and beautiful. He wasn't looking at her and yet, somehow, she knew He could see her.

---

[30] John 8:7

She cannot make out what He is writing. She would have to lift her head and open her eyes wide for that and she does not want to draw the attention. The religious leaders are badgering Him, demanding that He make a judgement.

When they kept on questioning him, he straightened up and said to them, "Let any one of you who is without sin be the first to throw a stone at her." Again he stooped down and wrote on the ground.[31]

"Without sin?" She closes her eyes again. These were the religious leaders; the teachers of the law. They were not like her. They did not sin. She braced herself for the volley of stones that would come her way. But all she hears is the muffled sound of stones being dropped onto the soft earth and the shuffle of feet quietly walking away.

At this, those who heard began to go away one at a time, the older ones first, until only Jesus was left, with the woman still standing there. Jesus straightened up and asked her, "Woman, where are they? Has no one condemned you?"[32]

For the first time, she lifts her head and looks around. They are all gone and she is alone with Jesus.

"No one, sir," she said.

No one! She was going to die today but now she has been given a new life. She was born again. She held her breath. Jesus was still here and if anyone had the authority to condemn her, it was Him. Would He?

"Then neither do I condemn you," Jesus declared.

She might have exhaled in sheer relief, looking up into Jesus' face for the first time. Tears began to sting her eyes even as she tried to hold them back. The cold, callousness of her marriage that sent

---

[31] John 8:7-8
[32] John 8:9-10

her into the arms of another man was the same cold, callousness of the Pharisees. But this time it sent her into the arms of Jesus. Not for sex but for real love.

But Jesus wasn't finished. *"Go now and leave your life of sin."*[33]

"Go and sin no more.[34]*"* Leave your sin behind. Don't take it with you. If you don't change anything, then things won't change.

~ *If you don't change anything, then things won't change.* ~

Even though the Pharisees were using her to trap Jesus, she really did commit adultery. Jesus said, "Leave your life of sin." He was not excusing her behavior. Jesus rescued us by dying on the cross for our sins. He exchanged His perfect life for our lives of sin. To experience a new life, we must leave our old life behind.

I wonder about this woman the most. Like the others, the Bible doesn't tell us what happened afterward.

Jesus said, "Go." Go where? Did she go home to her husband? How did he treat her after that? Did he kick her out or forgive her? What about friends and family? This was no private affair. Everyone knew now. How did they treat her afterward? What happened to the lover who abandoned her?

Were there times after that when people were so unkind, so unwilling to forgive or forget, that she wished they had thrown those stones instead?

~ *Did she ever forgive herself?* ~

Bad choices. We make them. We suffer the consequences. We seek forgiveness, promise ourselves that we'll change. Then make more. Each time we think it will be different. That we have

---

[33] John 8:3-11
[34] John 8:11 KJV

learned something - anything! And when we look back we see the twisted, smoking heap of a train wreck that is our life.

Jesus will heal us, forgive us and love us. But it is no guarantee that the people around us will do the same. We may have to live with the consequences of our actions for the rest of our lives. If we broke our family, it may stay broken. Our spouse may leave us. Our children may hate us. If you are living a life of known sin right now, stop. Turn to Jesus. The consequences will always be greater than the moment. And the longer it goes on, the worse it gets.

~*We cannot go back in time and change things.* ~

We might think that our society is above stoning someone to death for their sins. We're more civilized now but there is another kind of stoning that we do. And sometimes we throw these stones for far more trivial reasons than committing adultery. Sometimes it's for the way someone looks, or how they dress or maybe they just said the wrong thing or you don't like their Facebook post.

I like to imagine myself as the woman in the circle, kneeling in the dirt, her hands covering her face. But if I'm honest, sometimes I'm the stone thrower.

~ *Sometimes I'm the stone thrower.* ~

I judge when I should be loving. I think I'm better when I'm worse. It doesn't matter which side of the circle we are on. Jesus loves us and He offers us a chance to begin again.

Throwing Stones

They are throwing stones.
Not the hard gray ones
picked up from the ground
But the bigger heavier ones
Picked up in the heart,
Thrown straight from the eyes.
Rocks that come from their glowering looks
That say,
"I would never do that."
Or, "How could you?"

The stones smash against my soul
And pile at my feet
Spattered with my blood.
More rocks come from their tongues.
Sharp jagged ones
Like, "I'm so disappointed in you."
And, "You're worthless now."
They bruise my skin
And crack my bones.
They never miss.
I never duck.

A voice cries out,
"If any be without sin, let him cast the first stone."
They quietly go away
And I am left alone with Him.
He does not throw stones.
He offers forgiveness.
He heals wounds.
"Go and sin no more,"
He says.
I go
And He goes with me.

~ "Anyone who trusts in Him will never be put to shame."[35]~

He doesn't just wash away sin; he washes away shame. I cannot change my past or what others think of me. I cannot forget what others did to me or the things I have done to others but the sin and the shame have been washed away.

~ He has met me in the circle of stones. ~

He knows all about me and He loves me anyway. No price too high; no sin too great that He will not come for me. The most difficult thing is forgiving myself when others do not; to forgive myself when the ones I've hurt are still hurting. Even more difficult when they are my own children.

~The Lord has promises even for those times. ~

Jeremiah 31:15 – 17

This is what the LORD says:

"A voice is heard in Ramah,
mourning and great weeping,
Rachel weeping for her children
and refusing to be comforted,
because they are no more."

16 This is what the LORD says:

"Restrain your voice from weeping
and your eyes from tears,
for your work will be rewarded,"
declares the LORD.
"They will return from the land of the enemy.
17 So there is hope for your descendants,"
declares the LORD.
"Your children will return to their own land."

---

[35] Romans 10:11

What is your name?

All three of these women have one more thing in common. We don't know their names. I think they are unnamed because they represent all of us; all of our brokenness, all of our yearnings, all of our needs.

But they do have a name; a name that represents all of us. It's my name. It's your name. And it's this name:

"because you are called an outcast, <u>Zion</u> for whom no one cares."[36]

"<u>Zion</u> stretches out her hands, but there is no one to comfort her."[37]

~ Zion ~

The one for whom no one cares. The one who yearns for healing, love and forgiveness and there is no one to comfort her. I am a Zion. Are you?

~ God has a promise for Zion. ~

The Lord will surely comfort Zion and will look with compassion on all her ruins; he will make her deserts like Eden, her wastelands like the garden of the Lord. Joy and gladness will be found in her, thanksgiving and the sound of singing.[38]

You will arise and have compassion on Zion, for it is time to show favor to her; the appointed time has come.[39]

Zion, you are not alone. You are not unloved. You are not beyond forgiveness. He feels you touch His robe. He meets you at the well. He stands with you in the circle of stones.

---

[36] Jeremiah 30:17
[37] Lamentations 1:17
[38] Isaiah 51:3
[39] Psalm 102:13

Desperate women. Desperate for healing. Desperate for love. Desperate for forgiveness.

All three of those women were desperate for restoration. But the good news is all three of those women were <u>destined</u> for restoration. I am destined for restoration. You are destined for restoration. We are all destined for restoration. And Jesus is the great restorer. But there's more!

In Ephesians 1:11 it says, *"In Him we were also chosen, having been predestined according to the plan of Him who works out everything."*

You aren't just destined for restoration. You are predestined for it. He already knew. He chose you in all your mistakes and brokenness to be here on this planet. But more importantly, He chose you for redemption, mercy and grace.

"In the place where it was said to them, You are not my people, they will be called the sons and daughters of the living God."[40]

And one of my favorites. *"We all arrive at your doorstep sooner or later, loaded with guilt, our sins too much for us – but you get rid of them once and for all."*[41]

What is the need of your heart? Do you need healing? Do you need forgiveness? Do you ache to matter to someone? To be loved? Or have you faced a loss or hurt that leaves you so devastated you can't get out of bed? There is Someone who can restore. Why? Because He loves you. You matter to Him.

---

[40] Hosea 1:10b
[41] Psalm 65:2-3 The Message

I want to end with the most famous verse in the Bible.

~ *John 3:16* ~

"For God so loved the world, that He gave His one and only Son, that whoever believes in Him shall not perish but have eternal life."

A man named John wrote this. I thought it was his own words, but he was quoting someone else. He was quoting Jesus. And when I realized that those precious words came from His very lips of my Savior that verse became very new and very real again.

Imagine Jesus standing in front of a crowd. He's looking out at them and what does He see? He sees the blind and sick that He healed but who never came back to say thanks. He sees the people He fed who went away filled but came back for more; always wanting more. He sees the adoring people who would be in a different crowd just a short time later shouting "Crucify Him!" Those who would rip His beard from His face. Those who would put a bag over his head and punch him, then jeer and say, "Who hit you?" Those who would laugh while he was being beaten and his back ripped open from a nine-tailed whip. Those who would scoff when they laid His bloody back down on a plank of raw wood and hammer spikes into his hands and feet. They were all there in that crowd.

He stood in front of them, knowing their names, their past, their future, their sins and their victories. And He begins, *"For God so loved the world that He gave His one and only son…"*

Imagine Jesus standing here, wherever you are reading this, and He's talking to you right now.

"For God so loved the world" – how much? THIS MUCH! And Jesus stretches out His arms until His body makes a cross.

"That He gave His one and only son…" Perhaps He put His hand on his own chest when he said that? *"His one and only son…"* – hoping that someone picked up on it. HE was the Son!

"For God so loved the world" – how much? Spread out your arms and say it with me:

~ *THIS MUCH!* ~

"That He gave His one and only son, that whoever believes in Him shall not perish…

I know very well that you don't have to die or go to hell, to perish. I know what it feels like to perish – it's a weight on my chest that is always pushing down; it's to burn and hurt and be eaten up from within. That ache that gnaws and won't go away. It's to die a little every day. We go to sleep perishing, we wake up in the middle of the night perishing and we make it through our days perishing.

And Jesus says, "Whoever believes in me shall "stop" perishing!" The perishing stops right now. His Spirit will come into you and start the healing. He will quench the fire and stop the bleeding. He will end the addiction. He will heal the broken. He will forgive you! No matter what you've done. His blood washes away the sins that claw and burn and cause us to perish every moment of every day.

"Whoever believes in Him shall not perish but have eternal life." Perishing doesn't start when we die – it has been in us all along. And the everlasting life doesn't start when we die either. It starts the very moment we bow our head and ask Jesus to forgive our sins. If He can forgive the sins of those who put him on the cross[42], there is nothing you've done that is so bad that He can't forgive you. Jesus starts walking beside you on this journey that is everlasting life. It starts right now. The transformation begins now because YOU MATTER TO HIM.

For God so loved the world, that He gave His one and only Son, that whoever believes in Him shall not perish but have eternal life.

---

[42] Luke 23:34

Let me word that a little differently.

"For God so loved Zion, *the outcast*, that He gave His one and only Son, *the Savior,* that if Zion, *the beloved*, believes in Him, *her Redeemer,* she will not perish but have a beautiful, exciting and amazing life that goes on and on and on."

~ *That's how much He loves you.* ~

After

When all is done
Earth made new
Sin is gone
Our robes pure white
We've worshipped
Praised
Bowed down
Rejoiced
To our Creator
Savior
Father
Then
we will paint
some will sing
others dance
or sculpt
or build
Some will write
stories
songs
letters

Some will plant
roses without thorns
Others will climb
or swim
or soar
with eagles
We will hold
hands
caress
embrace
We will
play
laugh
comfort
Our tears will be
joy
After time ceases
there will be
time for
everything.

Acknowledgements

Many thanks. I couldn't have written this book without the support of my husband, Paul, who always gave me the time and space to write this book and many others. Thanks to my many friends who encourage me and pray for me. Immeasurable praise to my Jesus, my Savior, who is healing my grieving, sat down at my well and offered unconditional forgiveness.

Cover Photo: by Terri Blazell-Wayson
Author's Photo: by Eric Griffith

Thank you for reading this book. If you liked it, you may enjoy my other books available at terriblazell.com or Amazon.

Lisa's Testimony:
A Dog's Walk Through the 23rd Psalm
View Psalm 23 in a new way - through the eyes and heart of a dog. Join Lisa as she shares in her journey of faith and trust in both her master and her "Master Creator." Walk with her as she learns that some things can't be fully understood in this life and she must lean entirely on her understanding that her master loves her and all things are meant for good.

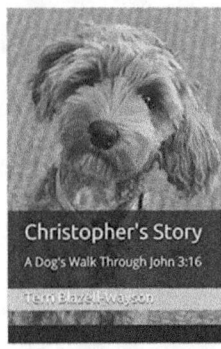

Christopher's Story:
A Dog's Walk Through John 3:16
Christopher weaves the beauty of John 3:16 through the tender story of his life from the first time he met his broken, human family to when he must say good bye. What does Jesus know about our lives here on earth? What can He know about addiction? A broken marriage? Abuse? As Christopher tells it, more than we ever realized.

Words for Women Who Hurt *and* **Words for Women Who Hurt Small Group Study Guide.**
Words for Women Who Hurt spills off the pages with a message of hope and healing to those who are hurt and broken from the things that life throws at us; our past, our relationships, the choices we've made and just plain life. Dig deeper with the study guide. It can be used individually for journaling or in a small group.

www.ingramcontent.com/pod-product-compliance
Lightning Source LLC
Chambersburg PA
CBHW072046170626
46811CB00008B/3190